A JIGSAW JONES MYSTERY®

The Case of the Snowboarding Superstar

Read all the Jigsaw Jones Mysteries!

- ☐ #1 The Case of Hermie the Missing Hamster
- ☐ #2 The Case of the Christmas Snowman
- ☐ #3 The Case of the Secret Valentine
- ☐ #4 The Case of the Spooky Sleepover
- ☐ #5 The Case of the Stolen Baseball Cards
- ☐ #6 The Case of the Mummy Mystery
- ☐ #7 The Case of the Runaway Dog
- ☐ #8 The Case of the Great Sled Race
- ☐ #9 The Case of the Stinky Science Project
- ☐ #10 The Case of the Ghostwriter
- ☐ #11 The Case of the Marshmallow Monster
- ☐ #12 The Case of the Class Clown
- ☐ #13 The Case of the Detective in Disguise
- ☐ #14 The Case of the Bicycle Bandit
- ☐ #15 The Case of the Haunted Scarecrow
- ☐ #16 The Case of the Sneaker Sneak
- ☐ #17 The Case of the Disappearing Dinosaur
- ☐ #18 The Case of the Bear Scare

- ☐ #19 The Case of the Golden Key
- ☐ #20 The Case of the Race Against Time
- ☐ #21 The Case of the Rainy-Day Mystery
- ☐ #22 The Case of the Best Pet Ever
- ☐ #23 The Case of the Perfect Prank
- ☐ #24 The Case of the Glow-in-the-Dark Ghost
- ☐ #25 The Case of the Vanishing Painting
- ☐ #26 The Case of the Double-Trouble Detectives
- ☐ #27 The Case of the Frog-jumping Contest
- ☐ #28 The Case of the Food Fight
- ☐ #29 The Case of the Snowboarding Superstar

And Don't Miss . . .

- ☐ JIGSAW JONES SUPER SPECIAL #1
  The Case of the Buried Treasure
- ☐ JIGSAW JONES SUPER SPECIAL #2
  The Case of the Million-Dollar Mystery
- ☐ JIGSAW JONES SUPER SPECIAL #3
  The Case of the Missing Falcon

The Case of the Snowboarding Superstar

by James Preller
illustrated by Jamie Smith
cover illustration by R. W. Alley

SCHOLASTIC INC.
New York Toronto London Auckland Sydney
Mexico City New Delhi Hong Kong Buenos Aires

For all the fan mail I've received.
For everyone who has read even one of the books in this series. This one's for you.
Thanks.
— JP

ISBN-13: 978-0-439-79395-7
ISBN-10: 0-439-79395-5

12 11 10 9 10 11 12 13/0

Printed in the U.S.A. 40
First printing, January 2006

CONTENTS

Chapter One

Wack Attack

It was the night before winter break, and my family was getting ready for our big ski vacation. I was excited. Or, as my brothers kept saying, *stoked.* My parents had already signed us up for snowboarding lessons. So I sat with my brothers Daniel and Nick as we went over last-minute details.

"Okay, I think I've got it," I said. "If a snowboarder says that something is *sick* . . ."

". . . that means it's really, really good," Daniel said.

"Sick is good," I confirmed.

"Right," Nick replied. "If something is bad, then it's *wack.*"

"Wack," I repeated. "So, like, falling down would be *wack.*"

Daniel laughed. "Sort of. It's more like this. Let's say you try to *bust* a 360° *ollie* with a *fakie* grab, but you get too much *boost* off the *half-pipe* and you have to *bail.* That would be *wack.*"

"Easy for you to say," I muttered. "But I don't understand what you are talking about. Why do I have to learn a new language just to ride a snowboard?"

"You want to be cool, don't you?" Nick asked.

"Sure, I guess," I said.

"Then you've got to talk cool," Daniel reasoned.

"Let us quiz you, Jigsaw," Nick said. "What

do you call someone if you don't know their name?"

I thought for a moment. "Dude," I answered.

"Excellent!" Nick cheered. "What's a face-plant?"

"It's when you fall into the snow face-first."

"Awesome, Jigsaw," Daniel said. "Totally *gnarly*!"

"Gnarly?" I asked. "What's that?"

"It means very, very cool," Nick explained. "Do you smell me?"

I sniffed, confused. "What?"

"Do you smell me?" Nick repeated. "It means, do you understand?"

"Not exactly," I groaned.

"Don't sweat it, Jigsaw," Daniel said. "In a few days you will be shredding the pow pow."

"Shredding the what?" I asked.

"Riding down the fresh powder, the snow! Even if it is on the bunny slope!" Nick explained.

My brothers thought that was pretty funny. The bunny slope. What a riot. Yeesh.

I was glad when my teenage sister, Hillary, knocked on the door. "Hey, Worm," she said. "Mila is here to see you."

That's the problem with being the youngest in the family. People call you "Worm" and "Shorty." I didn't care. I was used to it. And I was happy to see Mila. I raced out of the room to find her.

Besides, hanging out with my brothers was too wack.

Chapter Two
Mila

Mila Yeh had long, straight black hair. She was my friend and my partner. We were detectives together. For a dollar a day, we made problems go away. Some problems were small, like a missing frog or a lost coin. Other problems were creepy, like a glow-in-the-dark ghost or a marshmallow monster. Together, we could solve any case. We were a team.

But today we were splitting up. For a week, anyway. I was going on vacation with my family. Mila was sticking around. In fact,

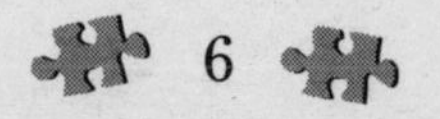

she was going to help Grams and my oldest brother, Billy, take care of our dog, Rags.

"I'm jealous," Mila complained. "I wish I were going on a ski trip."

"Snowboarding," I corrected her.

"It sounds hard," Mila said. "I hear that beginners fall down a lot."

"Maybe," I said. "But I think it will be sick."

"Sick?" Mila asked. "Who's sick?"

"Not who," I said. "*It.* Snowboarding will be sick."

Mila frowned. "I don't get it."

"It's the opposite of *wack*," I explained.

"Okaaay," Mila murmured.

"Do you smell me?" I asked.

Mila sniffed. "Well, now that you mention it, you do smell a little ripe."

"Hey!" I protested. "I meant, do you understand?"

"Not really," Mila said. "I think I'll stick with the English language, thank you very much."

We both laughed. I told Mila how my brothers had been teaching me the cool words I'd need to be a snowboarder. She replied, "I think you'd be better off with a helmet and knee pads."

I changed the subject. "While I'm away, you'll be on your own," I told her. "You'll have to handle any new cases by yourself."

"That's fine," Mila said. "I can always borrow Rags if I need some help."

"Or Joey Pignattano," I suggested.

Mila thought about that for a moment. "I think Rags might be more helpful," she joked. "Besides, I'll be busy practicing for my piano recital. I'm playing 'The Maple Leaf Rag.' It's a real knuckle-buster!"

"Well, good luck," I said. "I'll think about you while I'm shredding the pow pow."

Mila blinked. "I'm not even going to ask," she muttered. Then, brightening, Mila added, "Maybe you'll solve a mystery while you're away."

"Nuh-uh," I said. "No mysteries for me. This detective is taking the week off!"

"You never know," Mila insisted.

And she was right. You never did know. Because crime never takes a holiday. Jigsaw Jones, private eye, was soon going to be working on a new case. The Case of the Snowboarding Superstar.

Chapter Three

Superstar

The drive to Vermont lasted six hours. Think about the most boring show on television you can imagine. Like, I don't know, *The Wall Street Report.* Then imagine watching it twelve times in a row. While wearing a seat belt!

That was our drive to Vermont, but a little less exciting.

Yeesh.

The minivan was packed with:

luggage
snacks
two brothers (Daniel, Nick)
a sister (Hillary)
my parents (Mom, Dad)
and me (Jigsaw).

Grams and my brother Billy stayed behind to "mind the fort." That's what Dad always says whenever he goes out: "You stay behind to mind the fort."

Go figure.

Anyway, we were packed in tight like a hippopotamus in a Speedo bathing suit. Very crowded. Mom read to us from a brochure about the Blue Mountain Resort. It had tubing, snowshoeing, dogsledding, a game room — even a heated indoor swimming pool.

"There's going to be an Extreme Snowboarding Contest televised by EXPN,"

my mother told us. "The best snowboarders in the world will be competing."

That sounded cool to me. I had to admit, we got pretty stoked when we saw the snowcapped mountains of Vermont. Just sick!

After we checked into our rooms, we explored the resort. The place was huge. A lot of pink-cheeked people in bright clothes stomped around in heavy snow boots.

BLUE
MOUNTAIN

Clump, clump, clump. My mom kept clucking about how "rustic" it was. That was her way of saying that it smelled like sawdust and had moose heads on the walls. Poor fellas.

It was too late in the day to ski, so we gathered around a fireplace in a big open room. A large window gave us a view of the ski trails, the lifts, and the mountains looming high overhead. Snow fell softly from the sky, like tiny white marshmallows. Life was good. And so was the hot chocolate.

Suddenly a buzz of excitement filled the room. A small mob of people burst in through the main doors. They swarmed around one person, a gangly teenager with short black hair, sharp features, and dark eyes.

"It's him!" Hillary whispered. Her voice was dreamy and distant. "Lance Mashman, *Young Teen* magazine's number one hottie!"

"Number one hottie?" groaned Nick. "Who cares what he looks like? Lance Mashman is the best young snowboarder in the world."

"Second best," a voice sneered from behind us. I turned to see a tall girl with blond hair. She wore leather pants, red lipstick, and a sleeveless shirt.

She winked at me. "He's good," she said of Lance. "But this week he's going down."

Daniel and Nick were speechless. They

both stared at her, eyes wide. Hillary spoke up. "Wow, you must be Tara Gianopolis," she said. "Can I have your autograph?"

Tara scribbled her signature on a napkin. "Stick around for the competition," she said. "It's in two days. And I'm going to win it."

"Is that a promise?" Hillary asked.

"No," Tara answered. "It's a guarantee. I know his weakness."

"Oh?" I asked. "What's that?"

Tara glanced toward Lance, who was posing unhappily for a photographer. "You'll just have to wait and see." She sighed, and added, "I guess I should go greet the enemy."

Chapter Four

Unlucky Day

I wanted a closer look. Hillary and I got up to follow Tara as she strutted toward Lance Mashman. To my surprise, Tara marched up to Lance and gave him a big hug and a kiss on the cheek. Then she turned, with her arm around his shoulders, and smiled for the cameras.

"You'd never know they were enemies," I muttered to Hillary.

Hillary nodded thoughtfully. "Who's the other girl?" she asked. "The one hanging around Lance." Hillary pointed to a short girl who stood behind Lance. She was about my age and had the same dark eyes as Lance.

"She looks like his younger sister," I guessed.

By now, more and more guests of the resort had gathered around. They pushed closer, wanting to get a glimpse of the hotshot snowboarders. Tara seemed to lap

up the attention. Lance, on the other hand, looked like he'd rather be somewhere else. Probably alone on a mountaintop, I guessed, surfing on waves of white snow. The expression on his face said: "Anywhere but here."

"That's enough," a gruff voice spoke loudly. "No more pictures. Please, everyone, Lance had a long ride today and he needs his rest." The man waved his arms, dismissing the crowd.

Somebody backed up and stepped on my foot.

"Whoops, sorry," the photographer said in apology.

"It's okay." I nodded. "I walk on them, too."

He laughed. "That's a good one, dude. I'll have to remember that." He chuckled and held out his hand. "I'm Ace. I work for Johnson Snowboards. My company pays for this event."

"So what's with the camera?" I asked.

"It's digital," he explained. "I'll post the photos on our Web site tonight. Lance has a lot of fans. They love to see new pictures of their hero."

"Who's the big guy?" I asked, pointing to the loudmouthed man.

"That's Lance's business manager, Bubba Barbo," Ace replied. He looked toward Lance and frowned. "Hold on, something's happening." Ace immediately started clicking more photos.

"WHERE IS IT?" Lance hollered. He patted his back pockets frantically. His eyes searched the floor. "My lucky bandanna! Has anyone seen a black-and-red bandanna?!"

No one had.

Lance got more and more upset. He paced back and forth, searching the floor. "I had it with me. It was right here in my back pocket!"

I saw a smile sneak across Tara's face. She seemed to be enjoying this. Meanwhile, Lance looked more and more worried.

He turned to the younger girl. "Lily?" he asked. "Have you seen my bandanna? Did someone steal it?"

Lily was definitely his sister. Her almond eyes looked wide. She brought her fingers to her lips. "No, Lance. You put it in your pocket when we were in the car. That's the last time I saw it."

The burly manager, Bubba Barbo, barged up to Lance. "It's fine, Lance. We'll find it. Don't flip out."

"Don't flip out?!" Lance repeated. "That's my lucky bandanna. I always snowboard with my lucky bandanna in my back pocket. I can't compete without it."

"Sure you can," Bubba said. He rested a hand on Lance's shoulder. "I'll buy you a new one. Everything will be cool. Just chill."

"No!" Lance nearly screamed. His face was turning red. "It's NOT okay. You don't understand. I NEED that bandanna. I can't board without it! I have to find my good luck charm, or I quit!"

Chapter Five

A Working Vacation

"What's all the hullabaloo?"

I turned to see my father walking toward us. He said things like that all the time. *Hullabaloo*? Go figure.

"Lance Mashman lost his lucky bandanna," I explained.

"And he's, like, totally flipping out," Hillary added.

"Oh," my father replied. "I feel the same way about my credit card. Anyway, it's time to eat, kids. We have reservations in the Raccoon Room."

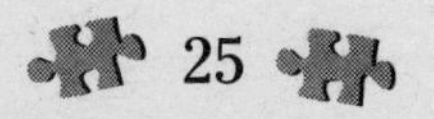

I told my father I'd be there in a minute. There was something I had to do first. "It's business," I explained. Once a detective, always a detective. Crime never takes a vacation—and neither do detectives. I handed Lance my card:

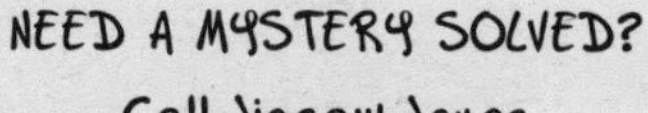

Call Jigsaw Jones
or Mila Yeh!
For a dollar a day,
we make problems go away
CALL 555-4523
or 555-4374

Lance looked at the card. "What's this?"

"I'm a detective," I replied. "Maybe I can help."

Lance just shook his head.

"You're upset," I said. "You can't think straight. Keep the card. I'm in room 247 if you need me."

NEED A MYSTERY SOLVED?
Call Jigsaw Jones
or Mila Yeh!
for a dollar a day.
we make problems go away
CALL 555-4523
or 555-4374

Lance shoved the card into his back pocket. "Yeah, sure. Thanks, anyway."

Just then his sister stepped forward. "Hi," she said. "I'm Lily Mashman. Nobody knows me, but I'm Lance's sister."

"Jones," I said. "Jigsaw Jones. I solve mysteries."

"So what are you, some kind of detective?" she asked.

"That's right," I replied. "The good kind."

Lily looked toward her brother. He was nervously running his hands through his hair. "How much do you charge?" she asked.

"One picture of George Washington will get me started," I said.

Her face went blank.

"A dollar," I explained.

She laughed. "I get it, George Washington. That's funny."

Lily told me to wait a minute. She had a quick, whispered conversation with Bubba

Barbo. I think he gave Lily a dollar just to get her away from him.

She handed me the money. "He's awful," Lily complained. "I don't like that man."

"No?"

"No, not even a little," Lily answered.

"Look, I have to go eat a raccoon or something," I told her. "Where can I find you?"

"I'm around," Lily answered. "I'm usually

tagging along behind my brother. Just follow the mob."

"Sure, whatever," I answered. "I'll snoop around. Ask some questions. See what's what. We'll talk later."

"Sure thing, Detective Jones," she said. And then, well, she might have given me a wink. Or maybe a bug flew into her eye. It was hard to tell.

Two seconds later I was racing to the Raccoon Room, hoping for a cheeseburger. I needed food if I was going to figure out this case.

Then it hit me: Mila! My best friend and partner was hundreds of miles away. We *always* worked together. But this time—for the first time—I would have to solve this case on my own.

Chapter Six

Learning the Hard Way

The next morning I had the first snowboarding lesson of my life. It was hard. I learned a lot . . . about falling. I didn't get hurt. But now I have bruises in places where I didn't even know I *had* places. I'm happy that snow is soft.

I was in the blue group. Like my brothers had warned, they started us out on the bunny slope. How embarrassing!

They had set me up with a short board, because those are easiest for beginners. The longer the board, the faster you go.

Since I could barely stand without falling down, I was happy to have the shortest board possible.

By the end of the day I started to get the hang of it. There was something cool about snowboarding. It was almost like floating on a magic carpet. Of course, then I wiped out. *Cowabunga!*

To make things worse, my brothers and sister were already snowboarding on the harder trails. "You'll get the hang of it," Hillary told me as she helped me up after another fall. "Just stick with it. Tomorrow will be a better day."

I sure hoped so.

Later that afternoon I found Lily Mashman in the game room. She was rolling up a big score on the pinball machine. But it didn't seem to make her happy. She looked bored.

"Hey," I said.

“Oh, hi,” she said, barely glancing up. She flicked the levers with expert timing.

I pulled out my detective journal. “Do you have a few mintues to talk about the case?” I asked.

She glanced at me, then back at the rolling ball in the pinball machine.

“The missing bandanna,” I reminded her.

“I guess so,” Lily finally answered. “I’m

bored out my gourd. And I'm starving," she added. "Let's go get something to eat."

We found a small eating area that was out of the way. I bought a large grape juice and Lily ordered a plate of curly fries. "How can you be bored?" I asked her. "This place is awesome."

Lily frowned. "For you, maybe. But with Lance on tour, my parents drag me to these places every weekend. We've been doing it for years. I'm sick of it."

"Don't you like to snowboard?" I wondered.

"A little bit," Lily answered. "But not too much. After all, my brother is one of the best in the world. I'm just the little sister who everyone ignores."

"Hmmm," I said. I grabbed a fry from her plate. That's another good thing about snowboarding. It even makes crummy fries taste delicious.

Chapter Seven

Suspect Number One

I asked Lily if the bandanna had turned up.

"Nope." She shrugged. "I guess it's lost forever."

"What's so special about it, anyway?" I asked.

"It's his good luck charm," Lily said. "My brother thinks he can't snowboard well unless he has that bandanna in his pocket."

"What do you mean?" I asked.

"He believes in luck. Like, I don't know,

he has to do things exactly the same way every time, or he gets all messed up," Lily explained.

I nodded, making notes in my journal. "Does he have any other lucky items?"

Lily laughed. "Oh, tons. I don't even know where to begin. He has a rabbit's foot that he keeps under his pillow. And he has to eat two bowls of Raisin Bran exactly one hour before his first race."

"Weird," I commented.

"No kidding." Lily laughed. "Lance always listens to the same song on his iPod before each race. If everything isn't perfect, he's a mess."

"Do other people know about this?" I wondered.

"Oh, yeah," Lily replied. "It's all over the Internet and snowboarding fanzines. My parents know, and so does everyone else."

"So," I said, looking into her dark eyes, "if someone wanted Lance to lose, maybe they'd take his lucky bandanna."

Lily sat back thoughtfully. "You think it may have been stolen?"

"It's possible," I said. "People do all sorts of things. If there's a thief, maybe I can catch him."

Lily rubbed her eyes. "I thought you were just going to help look for it," she said.

"I am," I answered. "But first, I'm going to need some suspects. I was hoping you could help point me in the right direction."

BLUE MOUNTAIN
SNOWBOARDING
FIRST
PRIZE
$10,000

Lily brought her fingers to her lips. "Sure," she answered. "I'd do anything to help Lance."

"I'm sure you would," I agreed.

"But why would someone want Lance to lose?" Lily wondered.

I took out a flyer I had found at the main desk of the Blue Mountain Resort. I unfolded it and flattened it on the table. "Read this," I said, pointing to the flyer.

"'First prize, ten thousand dollars,'" Lily read out loud.

I raised my eyebrows. "That's ten thousand reasons why somebody might like to see Lance Mashman do a face-plant into the pow pow."

I wrote the word SUSPECTS in my journal. Under it I wrote TARA GIANOPOLIS. "She's my number one suspect," I said.

Chapter Eight

On the Mountain

After asking around, I learned that Tara was at the top of the mountain, practicing her tricks. The competition began tomorrow.

To get up there, I had to take my snowboard and ride the chairlift. I'd worry about getting down another time. I was a detective and I had a job to do. I figured what goes up must come down. One way or another.

I watched with a small crowd of

onlookers while Tara performed some amazing tricks.

"Wow, she gets mad boost off the pipe!" one teenager exclaimed. I think he meant that she jumped really high. One rider kept taking nasty spills, falling again and again. "That guy is terrible," I muttered.

The teenager shook his head. "That's Lance Mashman. I don't know what's going on. It looks like he lost his skills. Dude, he'll never win tomorrow if he shreds like that."

I looked closer. Yes, it was Lance. He was having a tough time. Maybe there was something to that lucky bandanna after all. I also noticed that his manager, Bubba Barbo, stood nearby. Bubba's arms were crossed, his feet were spread, and he looked very, very angry.

I waited until Tara was finished, then I walked over to her with my snowboard under one arm. I handed her my card. "I'm

trying to solve a mystery," I explained. "Do you have time to answer a few questions?"

Tara lifted off her ski helmet. A cascade of golden hair fell down her shoulders. "You're that kid I talked to last night," she said.

I decided to take the direct approach. Sometimes you can surprise suspects and catch them off-guard. "I'm looking for the person who stole Lance Mashman's lucky bandanna. I figured I'd start with you."

Tara raised her eyebrows and grinned. "What makes you think it was stolen?" she asked.

"Without his good luck charm, Lance doesn't have any confidence. And you can't win without confidence," I told Tara. "With Lance out of the way, that ten-thousand-dollar first prize is up for grabs."

"Lance doesn't need a bandanna to ride well," Tara protested. "It's all in his head. He'll get over it."

"Maybe," I replied. "Did you take it?"

"Me?" Tara seemed surprised. She wasn't faking it. "Why would I steal from Lance?"

"He's your enemy. You said so yourself," I told her.

Tara thought that was really funny. "Lance and I have an unusual relationship," she confessed. "It's hard to explain. We compete against each other. We fight like wildcats. But" — Tara glanced around, then continued — "Lance is also my boyfriend."

"What?"

"He's my boyfriend," Tara repeated. "But it's sort of a secret. His manager, Big Bubba, would not approve. So we keep it quiet."

"But you two compete against each other," I said. "You are enemies. . . ."

Tara shook her head. "Man, you don't know much about snowboarders, do you? This isn't like football or basketball. We're athletes, but we're just trying to be the best we can be. It's about nailing a backside rodeo or pulling off a perfect McTwist. It's not about winning medals or beating people. It's about freedom and creativity."

"So you don't care if you win?" I asked.

"I care, I guess," Tara said with a shrug. "But as long as I ride well, I'm okay with whatever happens."

I believed her. Snowboarders truly were different. "One last question," I said.

"Shoot."

"Um, how do I get down from here?" I asked.

Tara's green eyes twinkled. She tilted her head and pointed down the long, slippery slope. "Down," she answered.

I gulped.

"I'll help you," she offered. "You can follow me. It will be like your own private lesson."

It was nice of her to offer. Except for one thing: I was scared to death. A question suddenly popped into my head. "Hey, do you have any idea why Bubba Barbo seemed so mad?"

"Well, you saw Lance out there," Tara said. She paused, then added in a whisper, "But maybe that's not all there is to it. . . ." Her voice trailed off.

"Go on," I urged. "Is there another reason why he'd be angry with Lance?"

Tara shrugged. "It's not my place to say.

All I know is that Lance and Bubba have been fighting for weeks. I think, um, maybe Lance fired him this morning."

"Lance fired Bubba?!" I exclaimed.

Tara threw up her hands. "That's what I heard," she said. "If you want to know the whole story, you'll have to ask Lance."

"Or Bubba," I added.

Tara pointed down the steep ski trail. There was a sign that had a black diamond. That trail was for experts only. "Are you crazy enough to try this?" she asked.

I hesitated. "Not really," I admitted.

Tara laughed. She pushed me playfully. "You'd be crazy for even *thinking* about it," she said. "Come on. We'll take the chairlift down together."

"You mean, I don't have to try to snowboard down?" I said.

Tara smiled. "Only if you want to die young."

"Um, no thanks," I replied. "Not today. I wouldn't want to miss my snowboarding lesson tomorrow."

Chapter Nine

Heating Up

I'll say this about riding in a chairlift: It's the only way to fly. The whole way down, Tara told me funny stories about learning how to snowboard. "I used to be a pretty good skier," she said. "Then some friends talked me into snowboarding. I could not believe how much fun it was. It was hard and I kept falling, but I LOVED it."

By the time we got to the bottom of the mountain, I felt sure that Tara was not the thief. She was too nice.

Lance was waiting for her near the rental shop doors. He gave her a little nod, like a secret signal. Tara turned and shook my mitten. "It was nice hanging out with you," she said. "Good luck on the case, detective."

"Yeah, you too," I replied. "Have fun tomorrow."

Tara smiled. "On that mountain? How can I *not* have fun!" Then she bounced off in the direction of her boyfriend, the

snowboarding superstar. They made a nice couple.

I had a lot of detective work to do. But first, I decided to go for a swim. My brothers said the hotel had a hot tub, too. After a day out in the cold, it was just what I needed.

The pool was warm and, best of all, nearly empty. I swam around, then sank into the hot tub. It felt like heaven. But the whole time, I thought about the case. If Tara didn't take the bandanna, who did? Or was I wrong about the whole thing? I'd sure feel foolish if we found out that it was buried in Lance's sock drawer. But I kept coming back to one thing: ten thousand dollars. That was some motive. And when there's a motive, there's often a crime.

Splash. I looked up and there were Lance and Tara. They were climbing into the hot tub to join me.

"I'm so sore," Lance complained.

"Rough day, huh?" I asked.

Lance grinned. "I had to bail on a backside rodeo 720. It was not pretty."

My bones were beginning to melt. That's the thing with hot tubs. They were awfully hot. I climbed out. Then I noticed another familiar face. Lily Mashman was sitting in a lounge chair near an older couple. I assumed they were her parents. Lily was playing with a Game Boy, but she didn't look like she was having much fun. Too bad. She wasn't a happy camper.

I walked over and sat next to her. "Oh, it's you," she said.

"Yep, me," I answered. We sat in silence for a few minutes. Her parents were pasting photos of Lance into a big, thick scrapbook. They didn't even look at me. I finally had to ask the question. "Why didn't you tell me that Tara and Lance were a couple?"

Lily shrugged. Her fingers went to her lips. It was a habit of hers. "I didn't think it mattered," she explained.

I grunted.

She put down the Game Boy and leaned forward. “I was thinking,” she said.

“Thinking is good,” I noted.

“Har-har,” Lily replied. “Seriously, though. I think it might have been Lance’s manager, Bubba Barbo.”

“Really?”

“Maybe,” Lily said. “He’s always kind of creeped me out.”

“Why would he mess with Lance?” I asked. “Doesn’t he want Lance to win?”

"They've been fighting a lot lately," Lily said. "Bubba wants Lance to sign on with a new sponsor. He could get a lot of money for it. But Lance doesn't want to."

"I don't understand," I said.

"There's a hair gel company called Goopy Stick," Lily said. "They want Lance to do commercials for them. But Lance won't do it. He says he doesn't like the way Goopy Stick smells."

"So what does this have to do with Bubba?" I asked.

"It's a lot of money, and Bubba would get some of it," Lily explained. "He's really mad at Lance for not taking the job."

"So you are saying that you think Bubba is a suspect?" I asked.

"Exactly," Lily said. "Lance needs to make money. Maybe Bubba thinks Lance will do the commercial if he doesn't win this competition."

My head was beginning to hurt. "I'll track down this Barbo character," I told her. "But it sounds far-fetched to me."

Lily smiled tightly. "Just trying to help, detective."

"Yeah, sure," I said.

I got up to leave. I needed to get back to my room and find my family. I had a lot to think about. And not all of my thoughts were happy ones.

Something about Lily Mashman wasn't right.

Chapter Ten

Big Bubba

"Whaddaya, kidding? I'm *glad* Lance lost that bandanna." I was speaking with Big Bubba, Lance's manager. He was on his way out the front door of the resort when I tracked him down.

"Lance doesn't need that thing to ride great. He could do flips in his sleep. But that doesn't mean I took it," said Bubba Barbo. "Lance drives me nuts with all his good luck charms. But you know what? They work for him. Do you know that Lance will only eat blue M&M's? He won't touch the rest of them, says they are bad luck. That's nutty, if you ask me."

"It sounds like you think he's annoying," I commented.

Bubba growled, "I don't *think* he's annoying. Lance *is* annoying. He's always late. He drives me up a wall and across the ceiling."

"You don't like him?" I asked.

Bubba made a face. "Whaddaya, kidding? I love the kid," he said. "Lance has talent. He's a genius on a snowboard. A great athlete. And besides that, Lance has heart. He's good people. You know what I'm saying?"

Yes, I knew what Bubba was saying. "I heard that he fired you this morning," I said.

Bubba stepped back, surprised. Then he laughed out loud. "Lance fires me every week and twice on Sunday," Bubba claimed. "It doesn't mean anything. We're a team."

Bubba's eyes narrowed. "Look, friend," he said. "I know that I'm gruff and rough around the edges. I know that not everybody likes me. But I'd do anything in the world for that kid. Lance knows that. It's why we stick together."

"Aren't you mad about the Goopy Stick hair gel?" I asked.

"Don't get me started on that," Bubba huffed. "Lance could get rich doing commercials for that company."

"And you'd make money, too," I noted.

"Sure I would," Bubba shot back. "I gotta eat, too. You think I do this job because I like standing around in the snow?"

He had a point.

Bubba looked at the front doors. "Look, kid, I gotta go."

I nodded. "Yeah, sure. Thanks a lot, Mr. Barbo. One last thing: When was the last time you saw Lance's bandanna?"

Bubba rubbed his chin thoughtfully. "That's the crazy thing," Bubba mused. "I saw Lance tucking it into his back pocket. He had a very special way of doing it. He'd fold it three times, just so, very carefully. When he put it into his pocket, Lance always made sure that a tiny corner of it would peek out. I'm telling you," he said, "I'm positive that Lance had that bandanna in his pocket when we walked into the resort."

"Very interesting," I murmured. Then I remembered one last detail. "Say, Mr. Barbo, do you still want me on the job?" I held out an open palm.

"What? You want more money?!" he boomed.

"I gotta eat, too," I countered. "You think I do this job because of all the swell people I meet?"

Bubba Barbo got the point.

And I got — wow — a portrait of Abraham Lincoln. Five bucks.

Before he walked out the door, Bubba turned back to me and said, "Just find that bandanna before Lance hits the slopes tomorrow."

Chapter Eleven

With a Little Help from Mila

After dinner I went back to my room. I needed to think about the case. What I really needed was my partner, Mila. So I picked up the phone and pushed buttons.

"Jigsaw!" Mila exclaimed. "What a surprise."

I told her about the case from the very beginning. I read from my detective journal. I didn't want to leave out the smallest detail. As always, Mila asked a million questions.

"Tell me more about the sister, Lily," Mila said. "Do you like her?"

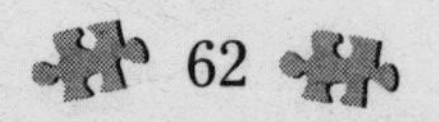

"She's okay," I answered.

"Is she funny? Friendly? Mean?" Mila asked. "I need more information, Jigsaw."

"I guess you could say that she's bored, mostly," I said. "I can't figure it out. This place is awesome."

I could almost hear Mila's Thinking Machine working on the other end of the phone. "Of course she's bored," Mila said. "Her brother is a superstar. Every weekend her parents pack her up to follow Lance around. Maybe she's jealous."

"I don't know," I said, thinking hard. "She seems to really love him."

"Well then, maybe she misses her regular life," Mila said. "I know I wouldn't want to have to travel around after my brother all the time."

"You don't have a brother," I pointed out.

"That's not the issue," Mila said. "I'm just thinking that maybe Lily has a motive, too.

It doesn't always have to be about money, you know."

I knew that. But, um, maybe I'd forgotten it. Mila asked me to describe the scene of the crime. I told her how Lance entered the room. All the crowds. The bumping and jostling. The big hug from Tara. Even the photographer from the snowboard company who stepped on my toe.

"There was a photographer?" Mila asked.

"Yeah, he posts all the photos on their Web site," I replied.

"What Web site?" Mila asked.

I didn't know exactly.

"Hold on," Mila said. "I'll look it up on my computer. I'll just type in 'Lance Mashman, photos,' and see what turns up."

I heard her fingers clicking on the keyboard. Then Mila said, "WOW!"

"What?!" I asked.

"He's cute!" Mila exclaimed.

er.

ibed the photos to me. She saw me pictures, she could see a bandanna hanging from his pocket. In other pictures, taken minutes later, there was no bandanna.

"So it was stolen right then," I said. "When everyone was around."

"Uh-huh," Mila confirmed. "There's a girl standing near him the whole time."

"Yeah, that's Lily," I told her.

Mila paused. Then she said, "Well, if you ask me, she's the one who stole it."

Chapter Twelve

Case Closed

The contest centered around the half-pipe, which was a huge tunnel of ice and snow. That's where all the boarders did their tricks. It was going to start in ten minutes. I kept searching for Lily, but she wasn't anywhere to be found.

Then I saw her, at the very top of the hill, standing near Lance. I greeted them. Lance was wearing earphones, listening to his iPod. It was like he saw me but didn't see me. I think he was focused on getting ready for the competition.

ily's coat sleeve. "We need to

y said. "It's about to begin."

firmly. "Now."

A look of alarm crossed Lily's face.

"You took it," I said to her.

Lily's fingers came to her lips. I recognized the nervous habit. She did it right before every lie. "What?" she said. "That's crazy!"

I smiled and tilted my head. "Maybe not," I offered. "You are tired of following Lance

around every weekend. You thought that maybe if he loses . . ."

I stopped talking. I could tell that I'd hit a bull's-eye.

"I just want him to be home sometimes," Lily said. "I just want my parents to notice somebody else besides Lance."

A hand fell on Lily's shoulder. She looked up to see her brother, the snowboarding superstar. His iPod was turned off. He had heard every word.

"I'm sorry, Lily," he said. "I didn't know."

Lily squeezed him tight. "It's not your fault," she said. "I just want to be special, too."

Lance smiled down at her. "You are special, little Lil," he said. "I couldn't do any of this without you."

Lily smiled faintly.

"You are my *real* good luck charm," Lance said. "Don't cry, Lil. I'll talk to Mom and Dad. It'll be okay. We'll work it out."

I walked away, watching from a distance. Just before the race began, Lily reached into her coat pocket. She handed Lance a black-and-red bandanna. He grinned, folded it three times, and stuffed it into his pocket. The smallest corner peeked out.

I watched the contest with my brothers, my sister, and my parents. Lance was amazing, doing all his tricks to perfection. But he only got the silver medal. Tara won the gold.

And that was the end of that. I guess detectives get to have a vacation every once in a while after all. For the rest of the week, I rode my snowboard every day. I got pretty good, too. But after a while, I was ready to go home.

I had a partner to thank.

About the Author

James Preller often draws upon his own life as a basis for his Jigsaw Jones books. Like Jigsaw, James Preller has a slobbering, sock-eating dog. Like Jigsaw, James was the youngest in a large family. His older brothers called him Worm and worse—yeesh! And so do Jigsaw's!

James and Jigsaw both love jigsaw puzzles, baseball, grape juice, and mysteries! But even though Jigsaw and James have so much in common, they are not the same person.

Unlike Jigsaw, James Preller is the author of many books for children, including *The Big Book of Picture-Book Authors & Illustrators*; *Wake Me in Spring*; *Hiccups for Elephant*; and *Ghost Cat and Other Spooky Tales*. He lives in Delmar, New York, with his wife, Lisa, three kids—Nicholas, Gavin, and Maggie—his two cats, and his dog.